THE KEY TO
THE PLAYHOUSE

THE KEY TO THE PLAYHOUSE

by Carol Beach York
illustrated by John Speirs

A
LITTLE APPLE
PAPERBACK

SCHOLASTIC INC.
New York Toronto London Auckland Sydney

No part of this publication may be reproduced in whole or in part,
or stored in a retrieval system, or transmitted in any form or by
any means, electronic, mechanical, photocopying, recording, or
otherwise, without written permission of the publisher.
For information regarding permission, write to Scholastic Inc.,
555 Broadway, New York, NY 10012.

ISBN 0-590-46266-0

12 11 10 9 8 7 6 5 4 3 2   5   7 8 9/9 0 1 2/0

Printed in the U.S.A.   40

For Eva Moore,
an editor with whom it is
always a pleasure to work

This is the key to the playhouse,
In the woods by the pebbly shore,
It's winter now; I wonder if
There's snow about the door?

I wonder if the fir trees tap
Green fingers on the pane,
If sea gulls cry and the roof is wet
And tinkle-y with rain?

I wonder if the flower-sprigged cups
And plates sit on their shelf,
And if my little painted chair
Is rocking by itself?

RACHEL FIELD

CHAPTER ONE

EVERY summer Alice Ann and Megan came to their grandmother's house to visit for two weeks.

They were cousins and they came together on the train.

Alice Ann had two small suitcases that matched. They were blue, her favorite color. She had yellow hair and blue eyes, and ever since she was very small her mother had always said: "Blue is your color, Alice Ann." Lots of Alice Ann's clothes were blue, and at home her room was painted blue and she had blue curtains and a blue bedspread.

Megan had only one big suitcase, which she could hardly drag along. She had not yet decided on her favorite color. She had asked Gran once, and Gran had said, "Why not pick green — that's my favorite." But Megan was still deciding. (She liked red pretty well. Or maybe purple.)

Gran always met them at the train station, and they drove back to her house with the windows of the car shut tight and the air-conditioning on, if it was a hot day. Which it always was in August.

At Gran's, Alice Ann and Megan shared a big bedroom right at the front of the house. They could look down and see the front yard and the side yard sloping to the woods. They could see the road to town and the house where the Hartney family lived. There was another house nearby, in the other direction along the road, but it was hidden by trees — which was all right, because it was a small plain house that needed paint and wasn't pretty, so it was good it was hidden.

Every summer they hardly took time to unpack before they were racing down the sloping lawn and into the woods that grew around Gran's house. It was cool suddenly in the dense shade of trees, and they ran along to see who would be first to get there, to the playhouse.

Their mothers had grown up here, and the little house in the woods had been their playhouse. Their grandfather had built it. He was gone now, but you could see all the love and care he had put into building the playhouse.

It stood by a shallow brook, in the shade of the trees. Alice Ann and Megan banged open the door and rushed in to see if everything was the same as when they left it last summer.

Gran knew they would go to the playhouse first thing. She always had a surprise there for them — a plate of cookies or a bowl of popcorn. She put flowers in the green glass vase in the middle of the playhouse table.

This summer the flowers were bluebonnets that grew by the brook. The treat was a plate of oatmeal cookies, neatly covered with plastic. And it was this summer, as they ate the oatmeal cookies, that Alice Ann suddenly feared there might be robbers in the woods who would come and steal

the pretty things from the playhouse.

"We're lucky everything is still here," Alice Ann said, looking around at the plates on the shelves, the ruffled curtains, the pictures Megan had drawn last summer and tacked up on the walls.

"We need a key to lock up," she told Megan.

There had never been a key to the playhouse.

"I guess Grandpa just forgot," Megan said. They agreed that was what had happened.

It was a thrilling thought — robbers in the woods. It made Megan shiver.

They ran back to the house to tell Gran about the robbers, and how they needed a key for the playhouse.

Gran was in the living room with the blinds closed to keep out the sun and her feet up on a hassock to rest her legs. She was drinking lemonade, and the ice made an icy sound on the sides of the glass.

Alice Ann and Megan came in breathless and hot from running. There was lemonade for them in the refrigerator, but they wanted to tell Gran about the robbers and the key first.

"Oh, I don't think there are any robbers around here," Gran said.

"There might be," Alice Ann insisted. She had set her mind on this and nothing would change it. "What if they came at night when we're all asleep and stole things from the playhouse?"

"That's right," Megan said. But she let Alice Ann do most of the talking. Alice Ann with her silky yellow hair and beautiful blue eyes.

Megan wished her hair was yellow like Alice Ann's, and smooth. Megan's hair was not any color, not yellow, not quite brown. It wanted to frizz up when rain came and it never seemed to grow. Alice Ann's hair grew so fast, you could almost watch it grow.

Alice Ann stood close to Gran's chair. "Please, Gran, can't we have a key? We really need a key."

So Gran laughed and said, yes, they could have a key.

And the next day a man came out from town

to put a lock on the playhouse door and give Alice Ann and Megan a brass key to open the door. They didn't have to lock the door; it locked by itself when it was closed. The key was just to open it.

"Or you can set the lock so the door will open without the key," he explained — but they didn't want that. They wanted the door to lock when they closed it. They would open it with the key when they wanted to get in.

They hung around the doorstep of the playhouse and got in the way while the man put in the lock, and they were very proud of their key when he gave it to them.

"Can you put a hook inside the door like Gran has in her kitchen, to hang the key on?" Alice Ann asked. Alice Ann thought of everything.

Gran believed if she hung her keys by the door, she would never forget and go off without them. On the wall by the back door she had a shelf for letters to be mailed and a hook for her keys. So she never forgot to take her mail or her keys.

The man didn't have a hook, but he pounded in a nail, just inside the playhouse doorway. Megan was a little disappointed that it was only a nail, but Alice Ann didn't mind. And she always called it "the hook."

When the locksmith was gone, Alice Ann and Megan went into the playhouse and closed the door. Now everything was safe from robbers. Later they planned to get a piece of twine from Gran and tie it through the hole at the top of the key. Then they could hang the key on "the hook" when they were in the playhouse.

"Who gets to keep the key?" Megan asked when they were through playing for the day and closed the playhouse door behind them.

"We'll take turns," Alice Ann said.

"Can I be first?" Megan begged.

Alice Ann looked at the key for a moment, because she wanted to be first. But then she said, "Okay, you can be first."

So Megan was the first one to get to keep the key.

"Don't lose it." Alice Ann had the last word.

CHAPTER TWO

THE key to the playhouse was of course important to keep out the robbers — but Alice Ann and Megan soon discovered a use for the key that was even more important.

It could keep out Cissie Wilson.

She was a fat girl who lived in the house down the road that was hidden by trees. She was big and clumsy, and Alice Ann and Megan thought she would break all their pretty dishes and bump into things.

Cissie had not lived in the house-hidden-by-trees last summer. No one lived there then. Gran had said, "That house is an eyesore; someone should tear it down."

But no one tore it down. Instead, a few months

before Alice Ann and Megan came for this summer's visit, the Wilson family moved into the house.

Mrs. Wilson did sewing, and Mr. Wilson worked in town. "He can't earn much at that garage," Gran said. She was glad to give Mrs. Wilson a chance to make some extra money sewing.

On the second morning of Alice Ann's and Megan's visit, when they were just finishing breakfast, Mrs. Wilson came to do some alterations on two of Gran's dresses. Cissie was with her, and Cissie's little brother, Royal. Cissie was supposed to watch Royal while their mother fixed the dresses. They were going to play in the yard.

Mrs. Wilson was a friendly-looking woman, and besides knowing how to thread a needle, she had a green thumb. "Everything Mrs. Wilson plants grows like magic," Gran told Alice Ann and Megan. "You must go sometime and see her flower garden."

"You girls come over any time," Mrs. Wilson said. Then to Gran she said, "Cissie and Royal are going to play in the yard. They won't be in the way."

"Or maybe they could go to the playhouse with Alice Ann and Megan," Gran said. She felt guilty that she had called the Wilsons' house an "eyesore," and she wanted to make Cissie and Royal welcome.

Alice Ann and Megan thought that was an awful idea. They didn't want Cissie in their playhouse. What if she sat in the rocking chair? She might break it. They didn't want Royal. He was hardly old enough to walk and talk, and his nose was running.

"Go along," Gran said cheerfully.

So Alice Ann and Megan had to take Cissie and Royal, even if they didn't want to.

Cissie held Royal's hand and pulled him down the porch steps. Her shoes were scuffed, and she had a hole in the heel of her sock. Alice Ann and Megan could see it, big as life. Her braids were held at the ends with brown rubber bands. "Come on, Royal," she whispered to Royal when he held back, "this'll be fun."

Alice Ann and Megan went first to lead the way. Alice Ann was thinking hard. When they got to the playhouse, she poked Megan with her elbow and said in a loud voice, "Oh, who wants to go in that old playhouse. Let's go see if Jimmy Hartney is fishing in the river. Maybe he'll let us fish, too."

Actually, Alice Ann hated fishing, but she couldn't think of anything else to say.

"Oh, that's a good idea." Megan nodded her head like a puppet on a string.

"By the river?" Cissie squinted in the sunlight. Royal tugged at her hand and tried to get away on his own, but she held tight. "I can't take Royal by the river."

"No, you'd better not take your little brother there," Alice Ann agreed with Cissie. "He might fall in and drown."

They all looked at Royal, barefoot and fussy.

"I guess we'll just go on back and wait for Momma in the yard," Cissie said. "C'mon, Royal."

As she dragged him away, he began to tug harder to get free. She picked him up and staggered along, back to Gran's house.

Alice Ann and Megan watched from the shadows of the trees until Cissie and Royal were out of sight. Then they hurried into the playhouse and closed the door behind them.

Megan — who had the key — hung it on the nail by the door so she wouldn't forget it when she left.

Alice Ann got her dustcloth from the table drawer and went around dusting everything in the playhouse. Even things that were already clean.

There was the playhouse table, in the middle of the room, and four chairs around it. In one corner was the rocking chair, with a wooden back and a green seat cushion. Three shelves made a sort of cupboard on one wall, and on the shelves were the pretty dishes and teacups and a fancy empty candy box that was for spoons. In a white china mug Gran had given them, Megan kept colored pencils for her pictures.

"I bet you'll be a famous artist someday," Gran had told Megan. "And Alice Ann can write the stories. You two can make your own books."

Last summer they had made up a book about a water-goblin who lived in the brook by the playhouse.

There was still plenty of paper for stories, and bright-colored pencils in the china mug. When Alice Ann's dusting was done, they sat at the playhouse table and Alice Ann began to write another book. "It's going to be a story about cats," she said. So Megan began to draw cats on her drawing paper.

This was the way it should be. It was *their* playhouse, and no one else should come stumbling about, breaking things.

It was very quiet then, as Alice Ann wrote her story and Megan drew her cats. Sometimes they could hear a bird call in the woods outside. It was a perfect summer morning. The brook was glittering with sunlight, trickling along peacefully.

Best of all, the door of the playhouse was tightly locked.

CHAPTER THREE

THE next morning Gran took Alice Ann and Megan into town. They went to the library, and Gran let them each choose two books.

It was very solemn in the library. Alice Ann and Megan picked out their books carefully.

"How are you today, Mrs. Greyling?" the librarian asked when she stamped Gran's card. It made Alice Ann and Megan proud that the librarian knew their grandmother.

When they got back to Gran's house it was time for lunch. Alice Ann and Megan made sandwiches, and Gran gave them chocolate cake and apples. They went to the playhouse with all those things in Gran's wicker picnic basket.

There was a thermos of milk, too. Alice Ann

got teacups from the shelf, and they poured milk into the teacups and pretended it was tea.

"We need a teapot," Alice Ann said. Now that she thought of a teapot, the cupboard seemed bare without one. It would be so much nicer to pour their "tea" from a real teapot than from a plastic thermos bottle.

After they poured their "tea," they put all their nice lunch out on the playhouse table and were just starting to eat when Alice Ann looked up and, through the playhouse window, saw Cissie Wilson coming through the woods.

"That girl's coming," she warned Megan. She got up and jerked the curtain closed so Cissie couldn't see in. Then they both sat very still at the table, with the milk in the teacups and the sandwiches and chocolate cake and apples.

After a moment there was a *knock-knock-knock* at the door.

Alice Ann put her finger to her lips; they must not make a sound.

Megan turned in her chair to look toward the door.

It was safely locked.

The key hung on the nail.

Nobody could get in.

But there was *knock-knock-knock* again.

Alice Ann and Megan held their breath.

After a minute, when no more knocking came, Alice Ann got up again and opened the curtain just enough to peek out. Cissie was walking away from the playhouse.

Megan slipped from her chair and went to stand at the window, too. Alice Ann opened the curtain wider. Cissie was disappearing from sight through the trees.

CHAPTER FOUR

Cissie came again the next day. No one was in the playhouse. She went around the side of the house and looked through the window. Alice Ann and Megan saw her as they came through the woods.

"She's spying in our window!" Alice Ann said, coming to a sudden stop. She pulled Megan back, and they crouched in the bushes by a tree and watched Cissie Wilson looking into their playhouse.

She was seeing everything. Table and chairs, rocking chair, the shelves with the pretty dishes, and the candy box of spoons.

And she stayed and stayed, looking and looking in the window.

Alice Ann and Megan stayed crouched by the bushes, like spies themselves.

At first it was fun, hiding from Cissie. It was like playing a game. But by and by Megan began to feel hot and itchy. She fidgeted; Alice Ann poked her to be quiet. Cissie might hear them if Megan made a lot of noise.

Megan fidgeted some more. She couldn't help it. Even Alice Ann began to get restless.

It was very quiet in the woods, and Megan was afraid she would crackle leaves or twigs and Cissie would know someone was there.

She wished she could take off her shoes and wade in the cool water of the brook.

Then Megan thought she might sneeze, and she pressed a finger under her nose. A bug flew by, and Alice Ann shrank back to let it pass.

The waiting went on and on.

Then at last — *at last* — Cissie stepped back from the window. She looked at the playhouse a last time, and then she went away.

*   *   *

After that, Alice Ann and Megan kept the curtains pulled closed at both of the playhouse windows all the time so that Cissie couldn't look in.

The next day she didn't come. Alice Ann and Megan worked on their book about cats.

"One is a magic cat," Alice Ann said. "He can change into anything he wants to."

"He can?" Megan was the one drawing the pictures. All her colored pencils were ready in the china mug.

"He can be a dragon sometimes," Alice Ann said. "Or he can change himself into a bird and fly away."

Megan thought she could draw a bird. She wasn't so sure about a dragon.

She bent over the playhouse table, her colored pencil in her hand. A red pencil, for the fire coming out of the cat-dragon's mouth.

They walked back to Gran's house after a while. It was Alice Ann's day to have the key and she swung it by the twine, watching it glint in the sunlight.

They had decided they really *needed* a teapot, and when they got to the house they went to Gran's pantry to look for one.

Gran's pantry was a mysterious place, a long dusky closet lined with shelves stacked with cans of food, plates and platters, flower vases waiting to be needed. Surely a teapot would be there, too.

"I don't see one," Megan said with surprise.

"There must be a teapot," Alice Ann insisted. There was so much in the pantry, she was sure if she looked hard enough there would be a teapot. She hoped it would be blue and gold, with a Chinese dragon painted on the side and a lovely curving spout, like a teapot she had seen in a picture.

But there was no teapot.

"Hello, girls — are you looking for something?" Gran was there suddenly in the pantry doorway.

"We need a teapot," Alice Ann said. She looked at Gran with disappointment. She had thought for sure Gran would have a teapot. Gran's house was so big and wonderful, everything should be there.

"For the playhouse," Megan said.

"I see." Gran nodded her head. She understood. But there was still no teapot. "I'm sorry, girls — here, how about this lemonade pitcher?" She took down a round green plastic pitcher with a thick handle and wide spout. "Will this do?"

It wasn't what they wanted at all.

"Never mind," Alice Ann said politely. "That's not really a teapot."

The telephone rang just then, and Gran went to answer it. Alice Ann took one last frowning look around the pantry. She couldn't believe Gran didn't have something as important as a teapot! Then, with Megan, she stepped out into the bright kitchen and closed the pantry door.

"It's your mother, Alice Ann," Gran called from the hallway where the phone was on a table. There was a chair by the table, and Alice Ann settled herself there importantly. Her mother called every day or so. Megan hovered close by.

Her mother would probably be calling one day soon. Mothers did.

That night in bed, Megan thought about the playhouse. She thought of it silent in the dark night woods, with the brook nearby in the moonlight. She had never seen the playhouse in the dark.

She thought about her pictures tacked up on the walls, and the nail by the door for the key. All in darkness. All in the nighttime. She was almost asleep when she heard Alice Ann say, "I don't think she'll come back anymore, now that she knows she can't get in."

"No, I guess not," Megan said.

They were safe from Cissie Wilson.

CHAPTER FIVE

Bᴜᴛ the next day *knock-knock-knock* came again at the playhouse door.

Alice Ann's head shot up. Her story of the magic cat was forgotten. Cissie Wilson was back.

"Shush," she whispered across the playhouse table. She put her finger to her lips.

Megan sat stiff, her pencil in her hand.

There was another *knock-knock-knock*. Then silence.

Alice Ann and Megan sat as still as they could. Alice Ann kept her finger to her lips. Megan kept her eyes on Alice Ann. Megan didn't even breathe one breath.

Knock-knock-knock.

Next they heard Cissie turning the doorknob, trying to get in.

Alice Ann giggled softly, hunching down at the playhouse table.

Then Megan giggled.

Did Cissie hear them?

There was only silence.

Was she trying to look in at the windows, where the curtains were closed?

Had she gone away?

At last Alice Ann got up and tiptoed to the door.

"If she's still here, I'll tell her to go away," she said boldly.

Megan stayed at the table, surrounded by the silence.

Suddenly Alice Ann flung open the door.

She was about to say *"Go away,"* — when there through the trees came Gran. She was smiling and waving as she saw Alice Ann in the playhouse doorway.

"Hello," Gran called. "I'm bringing lemonade. I thought you'd like some on this warm afternoon."

Cissie Wilson was sitting on the playhouse doorstep. A rubber band had fallen off one of her braids, and the hair was coming loose. She had a package of store cookies in her lap, and she got up when she saw Gran.

"Hello there, Cissie," Gran said. "You've got the cookies, and I've got the lemonade." She didn't seem to wonder why Cissie was outside and Alice Ann and Megan were inside.

Gran came up the playhouse step, and Cissie followed right along after her into the playhouse.

"I thought you weren't here," Cissie said. "I was waiting for you. I brought some cookies for us."

She put the package of cookies on the playhouse table, next to Megan's drawings. The top of the package was torn off, and a few cookies were gone. "I was waiting for you and I ate some."

"That's all right," Gran said. "Plenty left."

She took the thermos bottle of lemonade out of her carryall bag, and there was another bundle in the bag. She lifted it out carefully, a large bundle wrapped in layers of tissue paper.

"A surprise for you," Gran said. She unwound

29

the tissue paper, and there was a teapot.

"A teapot! A teapot!" Megan forgot about Cissie Wilson for a moment, and Alice Ann almost forgot about her — but not quite. Alice Ann thought it would have been nicer to get their teapot without Cissie hovering over it.

"I remembered I did have a teapot after all," Gran said. "It was packed away with some other things in the attic."

There wasn't any Chinese dragon on the teapot, but there were pretty pink flowers with dark green leaves, and a narrow rim of gold around the teapot lid.

Alice Ann and Megan passed it back and forth to admire it. Cissie watched. Nobody said she could hold it, so she didn't ask.

"Oh, thank you, Gran!" While Megan was lifting the lid to look inside, Alice Ann gave Gran a big hug. "I knew you had one somewhere," she said faithfully.

"Well, then, how about some cups and a plate for the cookies," Gran said.

Alice Ann bustled to the cupboard shelves. She had to get four cups, because Cissie had got into the playhouse.

While Gran poured the lemonade into the teapot, Megan found a plate for the cookies.

"Here we go," Gran said. She poured the ice-cold lemonade into the four cups, and Cissie turned her cookie bag upside down and poured the cookies onto the plate. Several bounced off and fell on the floor.

"Oh — " Cissie said. She picked them up and tried to dust them off.

"Don't bother, Cissie." Gran shook her head quickly. "Let's give those to the birds." She didn't want to eat cookies that had dropped on the floor.

Alice Ann and Megan rolled their eyes. *They* would not be dumb enough to spill cookies like that — or dumb enough to try to clean them off afterwards. They watched fearfully as Gran gave Cissie a cup of lemonade. She took it in her clumsy hands. But she didn't drop it or break it — not yet, anyway, Alice Ann thought.

"What are you girls working on?" Gran asked. She looked down at the table where the cat drawings were.

"It's a story about cats," Alice Ann said.

"And these are Megan's wonderful drawings." Gran sipped her lemonade and picked up the top drawing sheet to look at it more closely.

Alice Ann glanced out of the corner of her eye. Cissie was roaming around the playhouse, looking at everything, touching everything. She was *in* at last.

Oh, why did Gran have to come just then! Just when Cissie was on the doorstep!

"Those are my pencils," Megan said, when Cissie picked up the china mug.

Cissie put down the mug. Then she went to look at the dishes on the shelves.

She sat in the rocking chair and rocked herself. Fat and untidy, sloshing her lemonade on the playhouse floor as she rocked.

"Don't you have to watch your brother?" Alice Ann asked. She wished Cissie would go home.

"Not today," Cissie said. She ate a cookie, and crumbs fell in her lap.

"I must get back to the house," Gran said finally, setting down her empty cup.

Cissie went on rocking in the rocking chair as if she were going to stay forever.

Alice Ann and Megan looked at each other. They didn't want Gran to go and leave Cissie in the playhouse with them.

"We have to go, too," Megan said.

Gran took the key from the nail by the door. "Whose turn is it to keep the key?" she asked. "Cissie's?"

She turned toward Cissie and held out the key.

But Alice Ann stepped between them. "No, it's my turn today," she said. And she took the key from Gran with a tug.

Then they all went outside and closed the playhouse door. Alice Ann held the key tightly in her hand as they went through the woods toward Gran's house.

Cissie came along behind. Gran had put the

cookies that were left over back into the bag and Cissie carried that, swinging it in her hand as she walked along.

"Royal will like some of those cookies," Gran had said. So Cissie was going to take them home.

Chapter Six

THE next morning Cissie was back at Gran's house bright and early.

Alice Ann and Megan were sitting on the front porch steps watching birds in the birdbath on Gran's lawn. The birds flew down and sat on the bath rim, tilting their heads this way and that. Sometimes they rose up and flew off again without even getting wet. Other times they fluttered into the water with a swish of wings, sending droplets sparkling into the sunshine.

"I wish I was a bird," Megan said. She propped her chin in her hand and thought about being a bird.

She didn't see Cissie Wilson coming until Alice

Ann poked her with an elbow and said, "Look who's coming."

And there was Cissie, trudging along the road, turning into Gran's yard. It was too late to run away and hide. She had seen them.

Alice Ann and Megan sat where they were and watched her come.

She had on the same blue shorts she always wore, and an orange blouse that looked hot in the sunlight. Her hair was loose and hung in her eyes.

A last bird lifted up and flew out of the bird-bath. It was deserted for a time, with the sun shining on the water.

When Cissie was close enough, she said, "Hi." She slowed down and came to a stop at the foot of the porch steps.

"Hi," Alice Ann said, not too friendly.

Megan twisted a strand of hair and stared at Cissie.

"Are we going to play in the playhouse today?" Cissie asked. "I brought some stuff — " She took a handful of stubby colored pencils and crayons from the pocket in her shorts and held them out for Alice Ann and Megan to see.

"We're not going there," Alice Ann said. "We're going to help Gran bake a cake for her bridge ladies tonight."

It was a wonderful excuse. And it was true. They *were* going to help Gran make the cake. She said she'd call them when she was ready, and they were waiting. Cissie might as well go home; they weren't going to play in the playhouse this morning.

But just then, at just the wrong time again, Gran came to the screen door and said, "Time to start the cake, girls — oh, hello there, Cissie." She opened the screen door and came out on the porch.

Alice Ann and Megan started to get up from the steps. They had to go inside now. Cissie should go home.

But no. "We're going to bake a cake," Gran was saying to Cissie. "Why don't you come in and help us?"

And then Cissie was coming right up the porch

steps and into the house with them.

Alice Ann and Megan didn't like that at all. They wanted to help Gran by themselves, not with Cissie Wilson fumbling around. But there she was. When she sifted the flour, it got all over everything. Even Gran had to laugh and say, "Watch what you're doing, Cissie!"

Alice Ann beat the eggs. She measured the vanilla.

Megan stirred the butter and sugar together and got out all the lumps.

Only Cissie made a mess.

Alice Ann and Megan thought maybe Gran would get mad and tell sloppy Cissie to go home, but she only laughed and wiped up the flour. When Cissie spilled the salt, Gran didn't even see.

At last the cake was ready for the oven. It was a three-layer cake, and in went the pans, one-two-three. The oven door closed with a steely click.

They had made extra batter, and Gran poured that into a cupcake tin. The cake was for the

bridge ladies, but the cupcakes were for the girls to eat.

"Can we make the frosting now?" Megan asked. That was her favorite part. Especially tasting it and scraping the bowl afterwards.

"Not yet." Gran shook her head. "First the cake has to bake. Then it has to cool a while. We'll make the frosting after lunch. You can go and play now."

Alice Ann and Megan dashed away while Cissie was still trying to untie the apron Gran had given her. They were away like lightning, with the back screen door slamming behind them as they tore toward the woods and the playhouse.

"Wait for me," Cissie called, leaving her apron at last in a heap on the kitchen floor.

But Alice Ann and Megan were too fast for her. They dashed into the playhouse and closed the door.

When Cissie got there and began her *knock-knock-knock*, they stood just inside the door and held their hands over their mouths so Cissie wouldn't hear them giggling.

Megan wanted to shout, *"You can't come in!"* but it was more fun just to hide there behind the door and giggle with Alice Ann.

Megan began to giggle more and more.

"She heard you," Alice Ann scolded.

Then it didn't seem to matter anymore, and they both giggled as loud as they wanted to.

CHAPTER SEVEN

AFTER lunch, when the cupcakes and cake were ready to frost, Gran got out the mixing bowls again.

She had four bowls that rested one inside the other, from smallest to largest: blue, red, green, yellow. She had had the bowls for so many years, she couldn't even remember how many.

"Are they older than *we* are?" Alice Ann asked.

"Lots older," Gran said.

The yellow bowl was so big and heavy, Alice Ann and Megan could hardly hold it, and the blue one was too small for frosting. Gran chose the green bowl, and they began.

"I wonder where Cissie is," Gran said as they measured out the powdered sugar and cocoa. "I told her to come and help after lunch."

But Cissie didn't come back to help make the frosting.

When the frosting was all mixed up smooth and chocolatey, Gran let Alice Ann and Megan take turns spreading it on the cake. They made swirly lines with the frosting knife on the top of the cake. The lines were like a decoration. The sides of the cake were hard to frost, and Gran did that part. "Hard even for me," she said. "Frosting the top is more fun."

Frosting the cupcakes was easy, after the big cake. Megan kept sticking her finger in to get a taste, but Alice Ann only licked the spoon. She licked it clean. "Do I even have to wash this?" Gran teased when she saw the spoon.

They packed up a thermos of milk and four cupcakes to take to the playhouse to have a tea party. "Here — better take two more cupcakes," Gran said as they were getting things ready. "In case Cissie comes."

Alice Ann carried the plate with the six cupcakes. Megan carried the thermos and some pretty paper napkins Gran had given them. They were leftover from Valentine's Day and were covered with tiny pink hearts.

They went through the woods, slower and slower as they got near the playhouse. Maybe Cissie Wilson would be there, trying to peek in the windows or sitting on the doorstep waiting for them to come.

When they got quite close, they hunched down behind bushes and tried not to step on any twigs or make any noise as they crept toward the playhouse. When they got close enough to see, no one was there. The playhouse sat silent and alone by the little brook. On one side there was deep shade across the roof; on the other side sunlight was sparkling on the playhouse wall and the trickling water of the brook. A few leaves floated along on the water like boats going off to distant shores.

"Is she there?" Megan whispered. She was behind Alice Ann and she could only see a corner of the playhouse.

"I don't think so," Alice Ann whispered back.

"Let's wait. Maybe she's around on the other side."

They waited. With their thermos of milk and the cupcakes and the party napkins. Megan wanted to get right inside and eat the cupcakes, but they waited.

The brook gurgled along. The leaf-boats sailed away forever. Birds twittered and rustled in the treetops.

"She's not here," Megan whispered. Alice Ann agreed. They got up and ran to the playhouse — quick, before Cissie could suddenly come out of the woods someplace. It was Megan's turn to have the key and she unlocked the playhouse door as fast as she could. They didn't really feel safe until they were inside and the door was closed behind them.

It wasn't as bright in the playhouse, with the curtains drawn, but there was light enough. They put their things on the playhouse table, and Megan said, "Let's eat first." They were going to write letters to their mothers and fathers, but that could wait.

Alice Ann got the teapot and teacups from the

shelf. Megan poured the milk into the teapot, and then poured the "tea" into the teacups.

They ate their two cupcakes each, and then they ate Cissie's.

When they were finished with their tea party, they sneaked outside to rinse the teapot and the teacups in the brook.

It was a dangerous, exciting time. What if Cissie Wilson came along while the playhouse door was open and they were outside?

The cups and teapot got a very fast rinse.

The water was cool and clear as glass.

"Hurry," said Alice Ann.

"I *am*."

They tore back to the playhouse.

The door slammed shut behind them.

And they were safe again.

CHAPTER EIGHT

WRITING letters to their parents was mostly for fun. Alice Ann's mother kept calling on the telephone to see how she was. She called every day or so and talked to Alice Ann. Then she talked to Gran.

"Oh, yes, the girls are fine, having a fine time," Gran always said.

Megan's mother called, too, but not as often. *How are my goldfish?* Megan wrote in her letter.

Alice Ann wrote: *Gran is teaching me to knit.*

Gran was teaching both Megan and Alice Ann to knit. However, Alice Ann was the only one who was *learning.*

Megan was all thumbs. She got all hot and perspiring and cross when she had to hold the

needles and the yarn. The yarn got sticky in her fingers. It tangled around the needles. Large holes appeared in what she knit.

Alice Ann wasn't perfect, either. She was not ready to win any knitting contests. But she liked the feel of the smooth shiny needles in her fingers. She liked the *click-click* they made. She liked to look at the pretty colored yarn dangling down from the needles, and the round ball of yarn lying in her lap. She was already planning beautiful things she would knit when she had learned how.

I will knit you a scarf someday, she promised her mother at the end of the letter.

When they were ready to go back to the house, Alice Ann and Megan pulled the curtain open an inch or two at each window and looked to see if Cissie Wilson was around anywhere.

No one was in sight on either side of the playhouse.

"Is it safe?" Megan asked. She always trusted Alice Ann.

"I think so," Alice Ann answered slowly. She stared hard all around at the trees and bushes, but she couldn't see Cissie Wilson hiding any-where.

They gathered up the empty thermos bottle and the empty cupcake plate and their letters, and Megan got the key from "the hook." They opened the door just a crack and took one more careful look outside. No one was there.

Then they ran home through the woods.

CHAPTER NINE

AFTER the morning when Alice Ann and Megan giggled so loudly behind the door, Cissie Wilson didn't come back to the playhouse anymore.

Alice Ann and Megan looked for her every time they went there. They thought they might see her waiting for them, sitting on the playhouse step in her blue shorts and scuffed shoes, with the rubber bands loose on her braided hair, a hole in her sock.

But she didn't come.

"Where has Cissie been?" Gran asked one afternoon.

She had come to the playhouse to bring them some ice cream, and they sat together at the playhouse table to eat it. The trees shaded the playhouse roof at that time of the afternoon and it was cool there.

"Oh, she's around." Alice Ann moved her hand in the air vaguely.

"She's around," Megan echoed, nodding her head.

"I guess she's busy," Alice Ann added. She thought that sounded good.

"Maybe she helps her mother sew," Megan said. This idea came to her suddenly. It sounded like a real excuse. Better than saying Cissie knew they wouldn't let her in.

Gran was doubtful. It was hard for her to think of Cissie sewing with a neat needle and thread — Cissie who spilled flour everywhere when she made a cake, dropped cookies on the floor, sometimes picked up her little brother, Royal, upside down.

"There must be another reason," Gran said.

"She has to take care of her brother," Alice Ann reminded Gran.

"That's probably it," Gran said.

*   *   *

The days went by Alice Ann and Megan took turns with the playhouse key. They always kept a lookout for Cissie; that was still a good game to play. They picked wildflowers by the brook and put them in the vase on the playhouse table. They worked on their book about cats.

"They have big hats with feathers," Alice Ann said, "and when everybody is asleep, they talk and dance and have parties — "

"Wait — wait — you're going too fast," Megan begged, trying to draw cats with hats with feathers.

One night there was a great thunderstorm, and the next day the woods were dark and damp and mysterious. Another day they went with Gran down the road to the Hartney house for lunch. Mrs. Hartney was one of Gran's bridge ladies. She prepared lunch enough for a dozen people, even though it was only Gran and Alice Ann and Megan. "Pa and Jim will eat what's left when they get through fishing," Mrs. Hartney said. She was a plump lady and she liked to cook. Alice Ann counted seven cookbooks in her kitchen, all lined up in a row on the windowsill beside a flower pot with a cactus plant.

Mrs. Hartney's son, Jim, was home from college for the summer, and she talked about him a lot.

"He'll take you girls fishing sometime," she told Alice Ann and Megan. (Alice Ann made a face when Mrs. Hartney wasn't looking, and Megan laughed. Alice Ann had to give her a kick under the table.)

The only time they saw Cissie was one day when they were driving into town with Gran to return the library books. Cissie was walking out to the roadway from her house-hidden-by-trees, just as they came driving by.

"There's Cissie," Gran said. She gave a toot on the horn to say "Hello" as she drove by. Alice Ann and Megan leaned out the car window and waved, but Cissie didn't wave back.

She stood and watched as Gran's car drove past. But she didn't wave back.

Chapter Ten

AND so the wonderful two-week vacation with Gran drew to an end.

Alice Ann's mother and father came to have a weekend visit with Gran and drive Alice Ann and Megan home. The extra bedroom was all ready for them. Alice Ann and Megan picked a bunch of fresh flowers and put them in a vase on the bedroom bureau.

The room was perfect, then, and when they saw the car coming they dashed down the porch steps and ran toward it, waving their arms like crazy people!

"What a welcome," Alice Ann's mother said, trying to keep her balance as Alice Ann gave her a big hug.

Alice Ann's father carried in the weekend luggage and settled in a porch chair. Gran had iced tea and cookies waiting, and he was glad to see that. He sat enjoying the peaceful countryside through his dark glasses, sipping his tea.

"Come and see the playhouse — " Alice Ann dragged on her mother's hand. "Gran gave us a teapot! And we're writing a book."

"Come and see, come and see," Megan joined in, filled with the excitement of the day, the arrival of the car, the coming of company.

"All right, let's see the playhouse," Alice Ann's mother said. She didn't say she was tired from the drive and needed to freshen up. She just waved to Gran and Alice Ann's father on the porch and called, "We're going to the playhouse — back soon."

Alice Ann had one hand, Megan took the other. They pulled Alice Ann's mother across the sloping lawn and into the woods as though she wouldn't have known the way well enough herself. This had been her home when she was their age. The playhouse had been built for her — and for Megan's mother.

She let the girls pull her along. And when they got to the playhouse, Alice Ann told her about the key to keep out robbers that might be in the woods. Alice Ann herself unlocked the playhouse door. They all went in.

The sun was not bright that day, and it was rather dim in the playhouse room.

"Why do you have the curtains closed?" Alice Ann's mother asked.

"Oh, no reason." Megan twitched open one of the curtains (but not very far). She peeked out to be sure Cissie Wilson wasn't waiting to jump out from behind a tree and spy into the playhouse window.

Then Alice Ann's mother forgot about the curtains. She admired the new teapot. She read Alice Ann's story about the magic cats and looked at all of Megan's pictures.

"Wonderful, wonderful," she kept saying. She was a perfect visitor.

When they came out of the playhouse, they took off their shoes and stockings and waded into the cool water of the brook. The bottom of the brook was stony in places, and the water lapped gently around their legs, not even to Megan's knees, and she was the shortest.

"What fun," Alice Ann's mother said, holding up her skirt to keep it dry. "Your mother and I used to love to do this," she told Megan. Long ago they had played in the playhouse and walked in the woods and waded in the brook.

They went back to Gran's house at last, walking slowly through the woods while Alice Ann's mother looked around and remembered things and listened to the birds twittering in the trees.

Gran and Alice Ann's father were still sitting on the front porch, and Gran got up from her chair when she saw them coming. She came to the edge of the porch.

"Why don't you girls go down the road and say good-bye to Cissie," she said. "Tomorrow is your last day, you know."

Alice Ann and Megan looked at each other

doubtfully. They didn't really want to say good-bye to Cissie Wilson. They hardly knew her.

"I thought you'd like to go say good-bye now," Gran went on. "You'll be busy tomorrow morning packing up and getting ready to leave."

"Yes, go along and say good-bye to your friend," Alice Ann's mother said cheerfully.

So there was nothing they could do but go to Cissie's.

CHAPTER ELEVEN

ALICE Ann and Megan walked as slowly as they could along the road toward Cissie Wilson's house. They didn't want to go there. Mrs. Wilson would be mad at them maybe, for not letting Cissie into the playhouse.

Maybe she would yell at them. Maybe she would tell Gran.

When they came to the path that led back through the trees to Cissie's house, they walked slower and slower. Leaves had already begun to drift down from the cottonwood poplars that grew there and hid the house from the roadway. Summer was ending.

They came to the house suddenly, through the trees. They could see Mrs. Wilson's flowers growing all around. Just like Gran said, Mrs. Wilson had a green thumb. Flowers grew close by the front steps, and all along the dirt walk that led up to the house.

The flowers were pretty, but they were the only pretty thing about the house. It was an old house, needing paint and looking shabby. The front porch had only one faded lawn chair set by the door. Royal's toys were scattered here and there.

No one was in sight.

"Maybe they're not home," Megan said hopefully. She wanted to turn around and go back. Alice Ann wanted to go back, too, but Gran had sent them to say good-bye.

They went up the steps and looked for a doorbell by the front door. There was none. The inside door was open, and Alice Ann peered through the screen door to see if she could see anybody. Megan knocked on the doorframe.

From back somewhere in the house they heard voices then — Royal's voice, for one — and footsteps coming along toward the door.

It was Mrs. Wilson herself. The last person Alice Ann and Megan wanted to see.

She smiled at them through the screen and then held it open so they could come in. Royal clung to her leg, his thumb in his mouth.

"Hello there, girls, nice to see you," Mrs. Wilson said.

Alice Ann and Megan looked at each other cautiously. Maybe Cissie hadn't told her mother about the playhouse. Mrs. Wilson didn't seem angry with them. She was as nice as ever.

"Now let go my skirt, Royal," she scolded. "You'll make me trip. Come in, girls — Cissie's here, out back."

"We came to say good-bye," Alice Ann said. "We're leaving tomorrow."

"Already? My, the time has flown." Mrs. Wilson smiled. "Well, come on then, Cissie's out back."

She led Alice Ann and Megan down a narrow hallway toward the back of the house.

They went through a kitchen and out to a small

back porch with unpainted steps leading down into a backyard.

On the porch Cissie was sitting in a kitchen chair, at a small table. On the table she had put a vase of flowers from her mother's garden. Next to the vase was a plastic cup holding her stubby crayons and colored pencils. A small bookshelf by the porch wall was lined with odds and ends of plates and cups. On the top shelf, like a place of honor, was a china teapot with a chipped spout.

Cissie looked up at Alice Ann and Megan, and then she bent over a paper she was drawing on, like they weren't even there.

"Cissie — company," Mrs. Wilson said. She didn't notice that Cissie went on drawing and didn't want company. Royal let go of his mother's skirt and toddled over to Cissie. She hauled him up on her lap and bent her head close over his head to keep from having to look at Alice Ann and Megan.

"Cissie was always talking about your play-house," Mrs. Wilson said cheerfully. She leaned against the porch railing and looked around at the porch. "She wanted to make her own playhouse — pestered me for dishes and a teapot and stuff, until she got everything she wanted. Except we didn't have a rocking chair anywhere. She said she needed a rocking chair." Mrs. Wilson laughed and shrugged. "But we had the other things. She lets Royal play here sometimes, but he breaks the crayons."

Cissie never lifted her head from Royal's. Her cheek was pressed close down upon it, and he sat silently in her lap, staring at Alice Ann and Megan.

It was hot on the porch. There were not as many trees at the back of the house, and afternoon sunlight fell across the worn boards of the porch floor.

"Cissie and Royal have tea parties out here," Mrs. Wilson went on. "Sometimes I come, too. Cissie pours the tea like a grand lady."

Cissie's head pressed closer to Royal. She didn't once look up.

"Well, speaking of tea parties," Mrs. Wilson

straightened up from the porch railing, "I could make you all some lemonade or something, and you could have a tea party right here in Cissie's playhouse."

"My mother's here — we have to go home," Alice Ann mumbled. "We just came to say good-bye."

"Of course it *is* hot out here," Mrs. Wilson said. "We ought to get some of those bamboo shades. You know, like they have on porches. That would make it nicer for Cissie."

Alice Ann was edging away. "We just came to say good-bye." It was like words she had memorized.

She didn't want to go through the house again, and she started down the back porch steps. Megan came close behind her. "Bye, Cissie," Megan said. "Bye, Mrs. Wilson."

"I'm sorry you can't stay." Mrs. Wilson followed them down the steps and around the side yard as they walked back toward the front of the house. Royal came trotting along after her and

she said, "Oh, here's Royal again. What a pest."
She picked him up and gave him a kiss.

But Cissie stayed on the back porch.

Alice Ann and Megan went back to the road
and walked along in the mid-afternoon sun.
There didn't seem to be much to say.

Finally Megan said meekly, "We could have
let her come in sometimes."

Alice Ann didn't answer. She stared straight
ahead as they plodded along. It was hot. A truck
drove by, stirring up dust on the road.

"Maybe next summer?" Megan said.

"Maybe." Alice Ann was still staring straight
ahead.

"Maybe next summer we shouldn't lock the
door anymore," Megan said.

They stopped walking then and stood together
by the side of the roadway.

Alice Ann had the key in her pocket. She took
it out and held it with the bit of twine dangling
between her fingers. They both looked at it, and
then Alice Ann put it back in her pocket. "Okay,

next summer we won't lock it anymore," she said.

They began to walk again, back toward Gran's house.

Next summer seemed a long way off. But it would come, by and by . . . and the playhouse door would be open.

ABOUT THE AUTHOR

Carol Beach York began writing poetry and short stories when she was seven. She still has the original plain brown composition book in which she wrote her first full-length novel, an adventure, at the age of ten.

Since then, Ms. York has written a variety of books for children and adults, including mysteries, fantasies, romances, and stories of the supernatural. Among her most popular children's books are stories about The Good Day Orphanage. *The Christmas Dolls*, *Good Charlotte*, and *Kate Be Late* are some of the series titles available in Scholastic paperback.

In addition to writing, Ms. York enjoys reading books, especially old books. It was in one such book, a poetry anthology, in which she found the Rachel Field poem (reprinted at the front of this book) that inspired this powerful and moving story.